TO:

_____

From:

_____

You are as bold as a lion.

New York Times Bestselling Author
Lisa Bevere

Lizzy the Lioness

Illustrated by
Kirsteen Harris-Jones

Tommy NELSON

A Division of Thomas Nelson Publishers

Published in Nashville, Tennessee, by Tommy Nelson. Tommy Nelson is an imprint of Thomas Nelson. Thomas Nelson is a registered trademark of HarperCollins Christian Publishing, Inc.

Unless otherwise noted, Scripture quotations are from the New King James Version®. © 1982 by Thomas Nelson. Used by permission. All rights reserved.

Author is represented by the literary agency of The Fedd Agency, Inc., P.O. Box 341973, Austin, Texas 78734

Illustrated by Kirsteen Harris-Jones

Tommy Nelson titles may be purchased in bulk for educational, business, fund-raising, or sales promotional use. For information, please e-mail SpecialMarkets@ThomasNelson.com.

Library of Congress Control Number: 2017937689

ISBN: 978-0-7180-9658-8

Printed in China

17 18 19 20 21 DSC 10 9 8 7 6 5 4 3 2 1

Mfr: DSC / Shenzhen, China / September 2017 / PO # 9448606

This book is dedicated to my granddaughter, Lizzy. I am
excited to watch your life unfold in courage and strength.
Never forget that in Christ you are as bold as a lion.
Love, Gmama

The righteous are bold as a lion.

PROVERBS 28:1

"Wake up! Let's go!"

The big lions were tired after a long night,
but busy Lizzy, the littlest lion, could not hold still.

**"Let's play! I'm hungry.
Look, there's a beetle. Let's chase it!"**

Lizzy bolted into the day. Busy Lizzy bolted everywhere.

Lizzy loved to hide low
in the grasses and then

POUnCe!

right on top of her friends!

She climbed the tallest rock and watched her shadow as it stretched across the African plain. She thought, *One day I will be big like the other lions!*

Just like you, lion cubs learn by playing. Lizzy loved to pretend she was a strong and brave lioness.

Lizzy didn't want to just **play** brave . . . she wanted to be **brave** like everyone else. But because she was little, all she ever heard was "be **careful**."

"Don't climb too high,"
an aunt warned.

"Watch out for that crocodile!"
her older cousin yelled.

"Stay within the circle
of our acacia trees, Lizzy,"
her mother purred.

Lions live in family groups called prides. Each day, Lizzy's pride walked its land to make sure it was **safe** from baboons and hyenas. Busy Lizzy wanted to go too, but she had to stay behind to nap with Nana under the acacia trees because Lizzy was still too little.

"We will be back soon," her mother said.

But soon never felt soon enough.

"I want to go!" Lizzy grumbled to Nana.

"I'm tired of being little!"

Sometimes Lizzy napped. Other times she didn't.
There was too much to explore.

As she inched away, Nana would say, "Hold that tail up
so I can see where you are at all times."

Lizzy climbed trees, **danced with butterflies**,
and played with the turtles that sunned themselves
on the riverbank.

One day, a sound tickled Lizzy's ears. It was like the stream
when the waters moved swiftly after the rains ... but different.

It reminded her of the call of the night birds.
The noise moved closer, but try as she might, Lizzy still
couldn't see what made it. So she climbed a tree.

She pulled down her tail
and crept out on a limb
to get a better look.

Closer. **Closer.** **Closer.** **AACK!**

The thin branch broke, and Lizzy fell on the ground right in front of a small girl wrapped in bright colors. The mother gasped, and the girl giggled. Lizzy scampered back to the safety of the tall grass.

Day after day, Lizzy peered through the grass and watched the girl with her mother. They filled the air with the sound of their laughter and songs.

She is little like me,

thought Lizzy, *and walks the land with her mother
just as one day I will walk with mine.*

One day Lizzy heard a different sound . . . one that **frightened** her. It was crying. A dangerous troop of baboons surrounded her friend, and the girl's mother was nowhere in sight.

"Dear God, please help me!"
the girl prayed.

Lizzy wanted to be **brave** and help, but she knew the baboons were bigger and more powerful than she was.

In that moment, Lizzy really hated being little.

In the distance, she heard the pride returning. Even though Lizzy was too little to fight the baboons, she wasn't too little to ask for help. **SWOOSH!** Lizzy ran through the tall, tall grass.

Lizzy found her family under the acacia trees. "The girl on the other side of the grass is my friend, and the baboons are taking her." **"She needs our help!"** Lizzy cried out.

As fast as the wind, the lions rushed through the grass and surprised the circle of angry baboons.

Her father's mighty roar shook the jungle.

"Roar!"

The terrified baboons ran away,
and the girl was safe.

Lizzy lay down next to her friend, and the lion family made a circle around them. The little girl stopped crying, smiled, and patted Lizzy's head. "Even though you are the littlest lion, you are the answer to my prayer," she said. Lizzy licked her hand.

The lions stayed until the people of the village found the girl. As they slipped away, Lizzy saw the mother pick up her daughter and hold her close.

"**You were brave today,**" said Lizzy's mother.

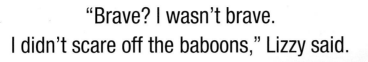

"Brave? I wasn't brave.
I didn't scare off the baboons," Lizzy said.

"You were also wise," Father said gently. "If you had tried
to save the girl, the baboons would have hurt you too.
You did the right thing by coming for us."

As Lizzy snuggled close, her mother said,
"Remember this, my little lion:

Sometimes the bravest thing you can do is to ask for help."

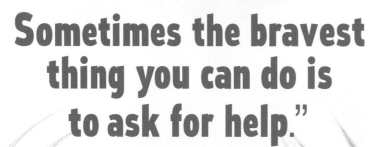

As a grandmother to my own little Lizzy, I am burdened that our children are sometimes seeing things that they don't know how to navigate. We, as parents and grandparents, need to have intentional **conversations** with them so that they can bring their concerns to us. I want children to know that no matter how little they are, nobody can take their **voices** away. Sometimes the most courageous thing they can do is ask for help.

Here are a few conversation starters to have those important talks with your child:

- *Have you seen someone bigger be mean to you or to someone else?*

- *How did that make you feel?*

- *Do you ever feel too little to help?*

Asking for help is not the same thing as tattling on others. When you see someone being hurt or in danger, asking for help makes you a hero. If you are frightened, asking for help is one of the most **courageous** things you will ever do.

- *Who are some people you can ask for help?*

Dear heavenly Father,

Thank You that You make me wise and as bold as a lion.

Give me the courage I need to do right and brave things.

In Jesus' name, amen.